Holly Berries of Christmas

Designed By Roni Akmon
Compiled By Nancy Akmon

To: *Lianne*

From: *Mom*

2006

Blushing Rose Publishing
San Anselmo, California

*Without strong
affection and
humanity of heart
and gratitude to that Being whose code is Mercy,
and whose great attribute is Benevolence to all
things that breathe, happiness can never be attained*

Dickens

Thy Saviour comes, and with Him Mirth,
Awake, awake!
And with a thankful heart His comfort take.

C. Herbert

The wind is chill;
But let it whistle as
   it will,
We'll keep our Christmas
   merry still.

Scott

Little town of Bethlehem,
How still we see thee lie!
Above thy deep and dreamless
sleep
The silent stars go by.

Yet in thy dark streets shineth
The everlasting Light;
The hopes and fears of all the years
Are met in thee to-night.

O morning stars, together
Proclaim the holy birth!
And praises sign to God the King,
And peace to men on earth.

Phillips Brooks

W E hear the Christmas Angels
The great glad tidings tell;
Oh, come to us, abide with us,
Our Lord Emmanuel!

Phillips Brooks

Like circles widening round
Upon a clear blue river,
Orb after orb, the wondrous sound
Is echoed on forever,
Glory to God on high, on earth be peace,
And love towards men of love --
salvation and release.

Keble

 HEARD the bells on Christmas
Day
Their old familiar carols play,
And wild and sweet
The words repeat
Of peace on earth, good-will to
men!
And thought how, as the day had come,
The belfries of all Christendom
Had rolled along
The unbroken song
Of peace on earth, good-will to men!
Till, ringing, signing on its way,
The world revolved from night to day,
A voice, a chime,
A chant sublime
Of peace on earth, good-will to men!

Longfellow

ARK! the herald angels sing,
Glory to the new-born King;
Peace on earth, and mercy mild;
God and sinners reconciled.

Hail, the heavenly Prince of Peace,
Hail the Sun of Righteousness;
Light and life to all He brings,
Risen with healing in His wings.

Come, Desire of nations, come,
Fix in us Thy humble home;
Rise, the woman's conquering Seed,
Bruise in us the Serpent's head.

Charles Wesley

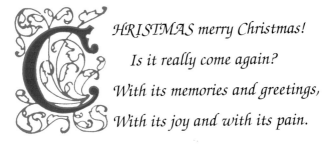 merry Christmas!
Is it really come again?
With its memories and greetings,
With its joy and with its pain.

There's a minor in the carol,
And a shadow in the light,
And a spray of cypress twining
With the holly-wreath to-night.

And the hush is never broken
By laughter light and low,
As we listen in the starlight
To the "bells across the snow."

F.R. Havergal

The time draws near:
The moon is hid; the
night is still:
The Christmas bells from
hill to hill
Answer each other in
the mist.

Tennyson

ITH such a prayer, on this sweet day,
As thou may'st hear and I may say,
I grant thee, dearest, far away!

Whittier

They bring me sorrow touched with joy,
The merry, merry bells of Yule.

In Memorium, xxviii

Though the snowflakes softly flutter,
And the frost be on the pane,
Though the wind or rain be sweeping
Over the bare and leafless plain;
Need we care for adverse weather,
When our warm hearts beat together?
Need we care for cold outside,
While our thoughts roam far and wide,
Waked by memory's touch again?

Helen Marion Burnside

 WEET Christmas bells, sweet
Christmas bells,
What happy tales your music
tells,

What memories of bygone times

Awaken when we hear your chimes!

The Christmas bells of long ago

Seem ringing over the world of snow,

And in your song again we hear

The voices sweet of yester-year.

Clifton Bingham

The dear notes ring
and will not cease,

"Peace and good-will,
good-will and peace."

S. Coolidge

OR on Christmas Day,
All are gathered above,
While mortals sleep the Angels keep
Their watch of wondering love,
How silently, how silently,
The wondrous gift is given!

Brooks

And like a bell, with solemn sweet vibrations,
I hear once more the voice of Christmas say, "Peace!"

The yearly course that brings this day about,
Shall never see it but a holiday.

Shakespeare

CHRISTMAS comes! He comes, he comes!

Gifts precede him, bells proclaim him,

Wet and cold and wind and dark

Make him but the warmer mark;

And yet he comes not one-embodied,

Universal's the blithe godhead,

And in every festal house

Presence hath ubiquitous.

Leigh Hunt

AM sending this small token
Of remembrance kind and true,
Just to bear a hearty greeting
'Neath the skies of wintry blue;
Just to wish that brimming measure
 Of the season's genial pleasure,
And the best of all good things
That the season ever brings,
 May be meted out to you.

So I send this little token
With the heartiest good-will,
Just to prove that I remember
 All who climb with me life's hill;
Just to prove that Time can never
Bonds of true affection sever,
That as years speed by we find
 They but more securely bind
Ties of "auld acquaintance" still!

       Helen Marion Burnside

S I drew my head, and was turning around
Down the chimney St. Nicholas came with a bound.
He was dressed all in fur from his head to his foot,
And his clothes were all tarnished with ashes and soot;
A bundle of toys he had flung on his back,
And he looked like a peddler just opening his pack.
His eyes -- how they twinkled! his dimples -- how merry!
His cheeks were like roses, his nose like a cherry;
His droll little mouth was drawn up in a bow,
And the beard on his chin was as white as the snow.

C.C. Moore

Be merry all, be merry all,
With holly dress the festive hall;
Prepare the song, the feast, the ball,
To welcome merry Christmas.

W.R. Spencer

H, the magic of the season!
How the golden love-lights shine
From sweet memory's fairy palace
In the land of "auld lang syne!"
How the snowdrifts' chilly whiteness
But enhances the warm brightness
Of the glowing Christmas hearth,
Gay with bright and kindly mirth,
As we watch the year decline!

Helen Marion Burnside

Rise, happy morn, rise holy morn,
Draw forth the cheerful day from night:
O Father, touch the east, and light
The light that shone when Hope was born.

Tennyson

The Wrong shall fail,
The Right prevail,
With peace on earth, good-will to men.

Longfellow

*The dark night
wakes,
the glory breaks,
And Christmas comes
once more.
O holy Child of
Bethlehem,*

*Descend to us,
we pray;
Cast out our sin
and enter in,
Be born in us
to-day.*

Phillips Brooks

O now is come our joyfull'st feast;

Let every man be jolly;

Each room with ivy leaves is drest

And every post with holly.

" Then sing to the holly,

the Christmas holly,

That hangs over

peasant and king."

George Wither

This is the month, and this

the happy morn

Wherein the Son of Heaven's eternal King

Our great redemption from above did bring:

For so the holy sages once did sing.

Milton

It is Christmas time;
And up and down
twixt Heaven and earth,
In glorious grief
and solemn mirth,
The shining angels climb.

D.M. Mulock

Designed by Roni Akmon
Compiled by Nancy Akmon

Efforts have been made to find the copyright holders of material used in this publication. We apologize for any omissions or errors and will be pleased to include the appropriate acknowledgements in future editions.

ISBN 1-884807-44-5

Blushing Rose Publishing P.O. Box 2238
San Anselmo, Ca.94979
www.blushingrose.com

Manufactured in China